From the wreck to the rescue this story is full of excitement and drama. We all daydream of living on a tropical island, building a house in a tree, exploring in a jungle and meeting strange creatures. All these incidents are here and lots more besides, and they all go to make up an ideal adventure story which children have enjoyed for over a hundred and fifty years.

Published by Ladybird Books Ltd Loughborough Leicestershire UK
Ladybird Books Inc Auburn Maine 04210 USA

Printed in England

SWISS FAMILY ROBINSON

Johann Wyss

retold in simple language
by Harry Stanton

with illustrations by Brian Price Thomas

Ladybird Books

Swiss Family Robinson

The storm had lasted for almost a week and it was getting worse. Our ship had been blown far off course and we were lost. Suddenly there came a cry of "Land ho!" – but at that moment the ship struck a rock and began to sink.

Up on deck we could hear the sound of shouts and running footsteps. I made my way up to the deck only to see, through the spray, the last of the ship's boats casting off! We had been forgotten! I rushed to the side and shouted, but the sailors could not hear my voice over the noise of the storm.

By now the ship was stuck fast on the rocks. It was no longer in danger of sinking, so I returned to my family to calm their fears. We spent the night listening to the storm, which gradually died away. Next morning all was quiet. The wind had dropped, and the sea was calm.

Since all the boats had gone, we would have to make one. We searched the ship, and found food, tools, guns and even some animals – two dogs, some sheep, cows, goats, hens and a pig were amongst them! My wife fed the animals while my sons, Fritz, Ernest, Jack and little Francis, helped me to make a boat out of planks and barrels.

Early next morning we launched our strange boat and slowly paddled to the nearby island. We called it New Switzerland, after our homeland. Tall palm trees swayed in the breeze and beneath them the grass was rich and green.

After offering up a short prayer thanking God for our safe arrival, we began unloading the boat. Later we built a tent from poles and a piece of sailcloth. While the children were collecting dry grass and moss for our beds, I made a fireplace using stones from the beach and lit a fire. My wife put a large stewpot on the flames and began cooking our dinner.

Then the children went exploring. Jack found an enormous lobster in a pool – or rather it found him! It grabbed him by the leg and I had to stun it with my axe. Ernest gathered mussels and oysters from the rocks, and later we used the shells as spoons. Fritz took one of the guns and went hunting. He came back with a small wild pig and the news that chests and barrels from the ship had been washed up in one of the bays.

That night we slept well. When Fritz and I went exploring next day with one of the dogs, called Turk, we found many strange plants and fruits. Some of the fruits were like large nuts and we spent some time making dishes and bowls out of them.

By mid-day we had climbed to the top of a steep hill from which we could see the whole of the island, which was much bigger than we expected. So much was growing that we knew that we would never starve.

In the swampy land at the bottom of the hill I discovered sugar cane growing. As we were gathering a large bundle to take back, a tribe of monkeys started to scream at us.

Suddenly I had an idea. Picking up a large stone, I threw it into the trees, and the monkeys flew into a rage and threw coconuts at us.

I picked up some of the nuts, Fritz gathered up the sugar cane, and we set off back to the family.

As we went through a wood we came upon a dead monkey with a live baby clinging to it. As Fritz knelt beside them, the baby sprang onto his back and held on

tightly to his hair. The baby monkey was very frightened and would not let go until I calmed it down by gently stroking it.

Fritz carried the little animal, but soon he got tired since we had so many other things to carry. Then he had an idea. He took a piece of rope and put it round Turk's neck, then set the little monkey upon his back where it rode all the way home.

The family were delighted with the things we had found, and they all loved our new pet.

My wife had a fine meal waiting for us She was roasting a large bird that Francis had killed, and she had made a huge pot of soup.

Next day we decided to return to the wreck, for there were still many useful things

aboard. My wife and the younger children stayed ashore while Fritz and I rowed back to the ship. First we fed the animals we had left aboard and then we searched the ship from top to bottom. We loaded our little boat so heavily that it sank low in the water.

Night fell quickly, so we stayed there until the following day. Our next problem was how to get the animals ashore, for we knew that they would not be able to swim all that way. After some thought, we tied small casks to them, pushed them into the sea, and towed them ashore behind our boat.

The animals were delighted to get ashore. As the boys and I struggled to take off their life jackets, my wife made an enormous omelette with some turtles' eggs she had found.

While we had been away my wife and the children had discovered some huge trees in which she suggested we should build a tree house.

It took us a long time to collect all the animals and to pack up our belongings before we set off.

The trees were the biggest I had ever seen. Since it was now too late to begin building a tree house, that night we slept in hammocks we had brought from the ship.

My first job next day was to make a ladder, for the lowest branches of the tree I had chosen were forty feet above the ground. Quickly I made a bow and arrow from some bamboo canes we had cut. My wife gave me a reel of cotton and I tied the end of it to the arrow. Then, taking careful

aim, I shot the arrow over a branch. A thin rope was tied to the thread and with this we pulled it over the branch. Now we could pull up a rope ladder.

While I had been doing this the boys had cut some thick bamboo to make rungs for our ladder. Soon it was fixed and we were able to begin making our tree house.

My wife and the younger children fetched wood from the beach while Fritz and I worked high in the tree. The work took us several days. At last our new house was complete.

That night we climbed up and I pulled the rope ladder after us. For the first time we felt safe as we slept.

As we ate lunch on the following day we decided to give names to the different places we had found. First of all we named the place where we had landed. After discussing it for a while, my wife suggested that we should call it Providence Bay. The spot where we had our first camp we called Tent House, then we talked for a long time about the name for our new home.

Ernest wanted to call it Tree Castle, Fritz wanted to call it Eagle's Nest, and Jack suggested Fig Town. To settle the matter I named it Falcon's Nest.

We named the stream Jackal River because we had seen jackals there, and we called the marsh nearby, Flamingo Marsh, after the birds who nested there. Lastly, we named the little island nearby Shark Island, since we had seen a shark near it.

Later that afternoon when it was cooler, the whole family set off back to Tent House where we were keeping many of our supplies. Fritz wanted some gunpowder and shot and my wife needed some butter from a cask that had been washed up on the shore.

We set off. The older boys and myself each carried a gun, while little Francis carried a bow and arrow. The dogs went in front with the little monkey perched on Turk's back, and a flamingo, who was becoming quite tame, following on behind.

Half-way to the beach Ernest called to us excitedly. He had found a patch of potatoes. We spent a while digging them up until we had filled our bags. Following the stream we found cactuses and rare plants growing, and to our surprise, hidden behind some rocks we discovered pineapples!

By the time we arrived at Jackal River and the beach, we had almost as much as we could carry.

At the beach everything was as we had left it. My wife went in search of the butter cask, and Fritz looked for the gunpowder. Ernest and Jack tried to catch the ducks and geese, but they had become rather wild and the boys could not get near them.

Ernest tied some biscuits onto a piece of string and threw them into the water. He pulled the biscuits closer to him each time the birds went to eat until he was able to capture them.

Carrying everything back to Falcon's Nest was not going to be easy, so I decided to make a sledge which could be pulled along by the donkey. The next morning Ernest and I collected pieces of wood from the beach and nailed them together. Two lengths of rope were fixed to the front and our sledge was ready. We loaded it with the cask of butter, a barrel of gunpowder and some tubs of cheese.

Half-way back to the Falcon's Nest one of the dogs ran off after a most unusual animal which bounded away from us. It was the strangest animal we had ever seen. It had an enormous tail and large hind legs but only small front legs. It was a red kangaroo !

As the wreck was still afloat Fritz and I returned to see what we could collect. We made several journeys to the wreck and on the last occasion Fritz found a sailing boat in the hold. It was in pieces and needed putting together.

It took us many days to build the little ship. When we had finished, it was so large that we had to blow a hole in the side of the wreck with gunpowder to get it out.

Our new boat had masts and sails and in the bows, two small cannon. We had a fine little ship!

Now it was time for another expedition to explore the forests. During the morning we found many strange birds and plants. After lunch we found some bushes that had very unusual berries which stuck to our fingers. They were candleberries. When we returned home we filled a saucepan with the berries and slowly heated them over the fire until all the wax was removed.

My wife made wicks from the threads pulled from a piece of canvas. These we dipped into the wax and let them cool until they had hardened. We dipped them into the wax many times until the wicks became thick candles. They burned with a strong, clear light. Now we would not have to go to bed at sunset.

Aboard the ship had been many young fruit trees which were to have been planted at the end of our voyage. Because of the wonderful climate the trees grew very quickly. We planted orange and lemon trees close to Tent House, and between there and Falcon's Nest we planted a long avenue of fruit trees. We hoped these would not only give us fruit, but also a shady walk protecting us from the fierce sunshine. Some trees with prickly branches we used as hedges to stop our animals from straying.

While we were planting and digging, we thought we would make our camps safer in case anybody should attack us.

Upon the tops of two small hillocks near the river I placed two cannon from the wreck. We had built a bridge across the river. Since it was very easy to cross we rebuilt it as a drawbridge so that it could be raised or lowered.

All these improvements took about six weeks, and our hard work had worn out most of our clothes. I knew that there were plenty of seamen's clothes on the wreck, so I set out with the boys. We spent several days removing chests full of clothes and anything else that could possibly be useful.

When there was nothing of any value left aboard I decided to blow up the ship. I knew that the wind and waves would blow the planks and timber ashore, and we could then store them for future use.

We rolled a cask of gunpowder to the bottom of the hold and to it attached a long fuse that would burn for several hours. We lit it and quickly returned to the island. After supper we climbed to the top of one of the hillocks. Just as it was getting dark there was a terrific explosion, the flash lighting up the night sky. The wreck was gone.

The next morning the whole family set off on an expedition as we needed many things from the forest. We wanted bamboo canes to support some of the fruit trees and as our supply of candles and sugar was running low we wanted some more berries, and sugar cane. We had made the sledge into a cart, so we harnessed the cow and donkey to it and set off.

We spent the afternoon picking coconuts and candleberries and cutting the sugar cane and bamboo we needed.

As darkness fell we built a shelter from branches and a piece of canvas. We would stay the night.

Then something upset the donkey; he began braying, then ran off into the forest and disappeared. We could not find him that night. The next morning Jack and I followed his trail for many miles until we came to some tall grass. As we pushed our way through it, we suddenly came face to face with a herd of wild buffaloes.

They turned and faced us. Those that were lying down slowly got to their feet. We were about to slip quietly away when our dogs burst through the long grass and seized a young calf. The buffaloes charged. We were terrified. Raising our guns we both fired, and the whole herd, except the calf, ran away. We roped the calf and led him along behind us. There was no sign of the donkey, and we gave him up for lost.

We arrived back with the family before dark to discover that Fritz had captured a young eagle. Young eagles can be easily tamed and we thought that he could be trained to hunt for us.

After staying at the camp that night we set off the following morning to Falcon's Nest. The young buffalo we harnessed beside the cow and the two of them pulled the cart.

The dogs ran on ahead, and suddenly we heard them barking excitedly. We rushed up to find our old sow which had disappeared a few days before. Beside her was a litter of six or seven piglets. We decided to leave the little family there and not take them back to Falcon's Nest until they were bigger.

One of our difficulties at Falcon's Nest was climbing the rope ladder. I was afraid that somebody would slip off and hurt themselves. My wife had noticed that the tree trunk was partly hollow. If it was hollow all the way up the trunk then we could build a staircase up to our home.

When I came to look at it next day, I discovered that the whole trunk was hollow. It would not be too difficult to build a staircase. To start with, we cut a doorway, and fitted one of the doors from the wreck. As the staircase was built I cut three windows. In three weeks it was finished.

At this time our goats had two kids, our sheep had five lambs and one of our dogs had puppies.

Gradually we trained our young buffalo to carry loads on his back. The boys also learned to ride him like a horse, and Fritz was busy training his eagle.

Our farm was getting bigger. The donkey returned one day bringing with him a wild ass which we captured and tamed, and our hens hatched out forty chicks. Now we had to build barns to keep the animals in, for the rainy season was coming. We had to gather in our winter stores, too, and plant crops which we hoped would grow in the wet season.

No sooner had we finished these tasks than the storms began. The howling winds tore branches off and drove the rain into our tree house. We had to leave, and we spent the rest of the winter living with the animals.

For the first time since we had been shipwrecked we were uncomfortable. With no proper fireplace we could not keep warm and the animals soon ate up their winter stores, so that we had to feed them from our own stores. The long nights and short days of winter seemed endless.

At the end of the winter we discovered that Tent House had blown down and many of our stores were ruined. Obviously we were going to need a safe, dry home for next winter. We searched for many miles along the coast, but we could not find a suitable cave. Then the boys suggested that we could dig a cave into the cliff.

I chose a delightful place overlooking
Providence Bay, and we began digging at
once. After two days we had not made a
very big hole, but the rock was getting
softer and easier to dig. A few days later
Jack's crowbar went right through the rock:
it was hollow! Quickly we made the hole
bigger. Inside we discovered a most
wonderful cave lined with crystals that
glittered and reflected the light of our
candles like a thousand diamonds.

This was to be our new winter home. We would live in Falcon's Nest during the summer and spend the winter in the cave. It was so big that we divided it into several rooms, cutting windows where we needed them to let in the light. Using wood from the wreck we worked for several months to make a very comfortable home.

While we were working on the cave, a great shoal of herring came to the bay. They were easy to catch, and we preserved some by pickling them in salt water. About a month later salmon began to swim up the river to spawn. They were too large for us to catch with lines and Jack tied a thin rope onto an arrow and caught some.

The first showers showed us that the rainy season was coming and we had not gathered in all the harvest. The next few weeks were very busy for us. By the time the rains came all the crops were stored away, the fields ploughed and the seeds planted for next year.

Our second winter was much more
comfortable than the first. During the winter
we made many improvements to the cave. I
fixed the great ship's lantern to a pulley in
the roof, and along the walls we made
bookshelves for all the books from the
wreck. Inside the unopened boxes we had
brought from the ship we found mirrors,
clocks and all kinds of furniture. Time soon
slipped by in Rock House, as we called it.

Spring returned and we set about repairing the damage caused by the storms. One afternoon Fritz noticed something coming towards us. Whatever it was made a great cloud of dust. All our animals were in the stables. It was something very odd. I went to the cave to get my telescope and I saw that the creature had no legs and had a greenish coloured body. It was a serpent!

The creature was enormous. We rushed into Rock House and pushed our guns through the windows. We were very frightened and no one spoke. Then as the serpent came closer, Fritz and I took careful aim, and we both put bullets through its head. With a great leap it rose in the air, lashing its tail about, then fell dead.

We wondered whether the creature had a nest anywhere. If there were any young serpents we did not want them growing up and attacking us. We had to look for the nest.

Two days later we set out in a great expedition to search for the serpent's nest and to explore the rest of the island. We set off like an army, with enough food and supplies to last three weeks.

We found no trace of any serpents, but as we passed the sugar cane plantation, we heard a rustling noise. The dogs began to bark and we raised our guns. From the sugar canes came a family of wild pigs. I shot two of them, for the little pigs would make fine ham and bacon. After skinning and cleaning one of the animals, we left it in salt water for a while before hanging it over a smoky fire until it was cured.

Fritz cooked the other pig like the South Sea Islanders do. He and his brothers dug a deep, round, hole in which they lit a fire. When it was well ablaze the boys put in large stones which became hot. Fritz rubbed the pig in salt, stuffed it with potatoes, and

wrapped it in large leaves. Then he laid it in
the pit and covered it with more hot stones.
He let it cook for two hours, and then
served us with a most delicious meal.

The next day as we continued our search, we found the tracks of the serpent, on the edge of a vast plain.

We crossed the plain until it became desert. From the top of a small hill Fritz called to me, saying that he could see horsemen. Quickly I looked through my telescope. They were not horsemen, but ostriches running in a line towards us! I watched them go to their nests, and decided to catch one.

I knew that ostriches could run faster than any horse. Carefully we crept up on the birds. The dogs were muzzled and Fritz's eagle had its beak tied up. We did not want an injured ostrich! As soon as the birds saw us, they ran away. The dogs followed them, and Jack released his eagle. It flew round and round the ostrich, making him run in circles. Then with one blow of its great wing the eagle struck the ostrich. The stunned bird stopped, Jack lassooed its legs, and the bird was our prisoner. From the nest we collected some of the eggs to hatch out when we returned home.

Our search for the serpent's nest continued for a long time but without success.

At last we returned to the cave and started to train the ostrich. This took several months. At first he was wild and would kick or peck us if we got near him. Gradually he became tamer until I was able to get him to carry small weights upon his back. Then I made a saddle for him, and he was able to carry the boys about at high speed.

Winter came once more and we had to stay in the cave. The days seemed very long at first, until Fritz suggested that we should make a small boat. He wanted to build a kayak like the Eskimos use.

We set to work, making the frame out of whalebones we found on the beach. Onto the frame we wove rushes. Next we covered the frame with seal skins which we sewed together. We made the seams waterproof with resin from a tree. I fitted a small seat inside and made a double-bladed paddle from bamboo. When it was finished we had to wait until the storms had died down before we could try the boat out.

Since Fritz had been the one to suggest that we made the boat, he had to be the first to take it out onto the sea as soon as the good weather came. When at last the sun shone once more, he was delighted to find that the kayak was fast and rode over the waves like a cork. We could not have made a better boat!

In the next ten years my sons grew up strong and healthy. Our animals multiplied and we started other farms further inland. On one of these we grew crops and on others we left animals which increased in numbers and grew fatter. Sometimes they were attacked by wild animals. Then we had to go out on expeditions to round up our own animals and hunt the beasts which had driven them away.

Now that my boys were young men they often went off on expeditions without me. Once Fritz went up the river in his kayak and discovered a great jungle full of colourful birds and animals. There was a herd of elephants which were so large that they were tearing down the branches of trees and stuffing whole tree tops into their mouths.

Further on he found sleek panthers padding through the forest, and in the river a massive hippopotamus which could easily have sunk his small boat.

On another occasion Fritz went on an expedition to explore the islands which we could see in the distance. When he returned his kayak was weighted down with furs. From inside his boat he brought out a bag full of pearls from an oyster bed he had found. Last of all he showed me a strange piece of cloth. It had been tied to the leg of an albatross that flew onto his little boat.

On the piece of cloth was written, "Help! Save the shipwrecked sailor on Smoking Rock."

Fritz had written a message and tied it to the bird's leg before it fluttered into the air and flew away. Somewhere we knew there was a shipwrecked sailor. Perhaps he came from the same boat as we did.

Now that we knew of the shipwrecked sailor, we prepared carefully for an expedition to find him, and also to bring back some more furs and pearls. Fritz made another seat in his kayak for the sailor he hoped to rescue. A large supply of food was loaded in the other boat and a week later we set off, taking the dogs with us.

We enjoyed an exciting day's sailing along the coasts of the islands and arrived just before dusk at the bay where Fritz had found the oysters. We landed and cooked our supper, then built a huge fire to keep off any wild animals. Afterwards we went back to the boat to sleep.

Early next morning we awoke and were soon gathering oysters. We left them on the beach where the hot sun caused the shells to open. The pearls inside were beautiful, although they were of little value to us at present. If we were ever rescued they would be worth a fortune.

Once again that night we lit a huge fire on the beach and left the dogs on guard while we went back to the boat. We were just about to go to sleep when an awful roar rang through the forest. Our dogs were terrified, and we were all frightened. We had never heard anything like it before. The roar came again, much nearer. Then a lion jumped from the forest into the circle of light around the fire.

He was the biggest lion I had ever seen, and the fire made him very angry. He came to the water's edge and crouched to spring at us. Then suddenly there was a shot. With a cry the lion leapt into the air, then fell dead on the sand. Fritz had saved us!

We could not sleep that night. In the morning Fritz went off by himself to search for the shipwrecked sailor. He did not

return that evening, nor did he come back the following night. We waited for another two days and then we went in search of him.

An hour later we struck what I thought was a rock. It was a whale, and it turned to attack us. Jack fired one of our cannon and it dived deep under the water. When the whale reappeared, Jack fired a second shot and it disappeared, this time for good.

As the boys were cheering, one of them sighted a strange man in a boat. We thought that we had at last met a savage.

I waved a white flag. He stopped and looked at us before paddling over to our ship. It was *not* a savage — it was Fritz with a blackened face! He had heard our guns, and had disguised himself because he thought we were pirates and he wanted to frighten us away.

Without another word he made us follow him to a tiny island. We went ashore and saw, through the trees, a hut made from leaves and branches. Fritz went inside and came out leading a young lady by the hand.

She was Jenny Montrose, the daughter of a British Army Officer. On her way home to England her ship had been driven far off course by a storm which had lasted for two weeks. The ship had sunk, and only Jenny had survived. For three years she had been living alone on a tiny island.

That afternoon we set sail for Rock House, stopping at Oyster Bay for the night before taking Jenny to our home.

Another rainy season came and went. One evening in the spring Jack and Fritz spent some time cleaning two of the cannon. Before they finished, they fired two shots. A minute later, as if in reply, came the sound of three guns booming across the water, but we could see nothing. We waited until morning, then we fired our guns again. A few minutes later came a reply. Seven shots sounded from out of the mist.

Fritz and I set out in the kayak, and searched for nearly an hour. At last in one of the bays, we found a ship flying the English flag.

We returned to Rock House and the whole family set sail in our little ship. The captain was surprised and welcomed us aboard. He had come to find Jenny, and offered to take everybody to Europe.

The family talked for a long time about going back. Life in New Switzerland was very pleasant, and my wife and I decided to stay.

It was a beautiful island, and we had large herds of cattle and flocks of sheep.

The boys had to make up their own minds. Jack and Ernest chose to remain; Francis and Fritz wanted to sail back to Europe.

When the captain and all the people aboard the ship came to visit us, three of the passengers liked the island so much that they decided to stay with us.

None of us slept very much on the last night.

At dawn the ship's cannon fired to tell the passengers to go aboard, and sadly we said goodbye to Fritz, Francis and Jenny, perhaps for ever.

"God bless," we cried, as the ship slowly sailed out of Providence Bay.

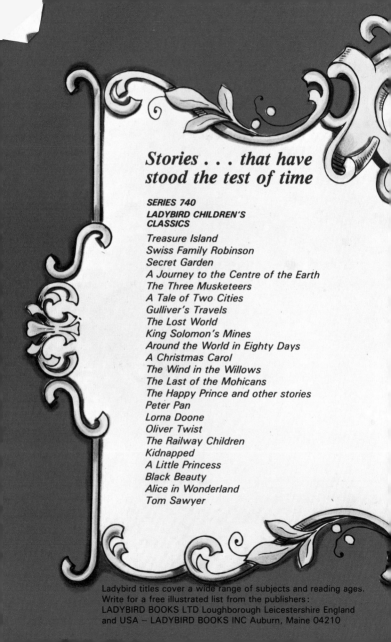

Stories . . . that have stood the test of time

SERIES 740
LADYBIRD CHILDREN'S CLASSICS

Treasure Island
Swiss Family Robinson
Secret Garden
A Journey to the Centre of the Earth
The Three Musketeers
A Tale of Two Cities
Gulliver's Travels
The Lost World
King Solomon's Mines
Around the World in Eighty Days
A Christmas Carol
The Wind in the Willows
The Last of the Mohicans
The Happy Prince and other stories
Peter Pan
Lorna Doone
Oliver Twist
The Railway Children
Kidnapped
A Little Princess
Black Beauty
Alice in Wonderland
Tom Sawyer

Ladybird titles cover a wide range of subjects and reading ages.
Write for a free illustrated list from the publishers:
LADYBIRD BOOKS LTD Loughborough Leicestershire England
and USA — LADYBIRD BOOKS INC Auburn, Maine 04210